Llamas On The Move

BY

JOHN C BURT.

This is the book called : ' Llamas On The Move?' It is concerned with a herd of Llamas and ...

their lives together in the Mountains of the Americas? The Herd of Llamas was ably led by one

large and majestic Llama by the name of Larry the Llama? Larry the Llama loved the air of the ...

Mountains ... Larry thought there was nothing better than the air of the Mountains for a Llama?

We in the following pages will look at some members of the Herd of Larry the Llama?

Larry the Llama's Herd was a Wild Herd of Llama's with some kinda human oversight ?

A rancher by the name of Jaybee loved nothing than to decorate the Llama's of the Herd of Larry!

There was a Llama by the name of Lucy the Llama who loved to meditate amongst the ...

15

very Cactus's! Then there was another female Llama by the name of Isabella the Llama...Isabella the Llama enjoyed hiding, if she could amongst the very green as green leaves of the Cactus?

There were two other Llamas who were part of Larry's Herd but they shall remain nameless to protect the innocent Llama's? Larry the Llama's Herd was a lovely Herd ?

Or at least that is what Jaybee the Rancher told all the other Rancher's; those who would listen?

Lightning Source UK Ltd.
Milton Keynes UK
UKRC011059120821
388404UK00004BB/86